HOW DO YOU LOVE?

THE FIVE WAYS WE SHOW WE CARE

Written by KELLIE BYRNES
Illustrated by MELINA ONTIVEROS

Feiwel & Friends
New York

A Feiwel and Friends Book
An Imprint of Macmillan Publishing Group, LLC
120 Broadway, New York, NY 10271
mackids.com

Library of Congress Cataloging-in-Publication Data is available.
First edition, 2021

Book design by Cindy De La Cruz

Feiwel and Friends logo designed by Filomena Tuosto

Printed in China by RR Donnelley Asia Printing Solutions Ltd.,
Dongguan City, Guangdong Province.

ISBN 978-1-250-77709-6 (hardcover)

1 3 5 7 9 10 8 6 4 2

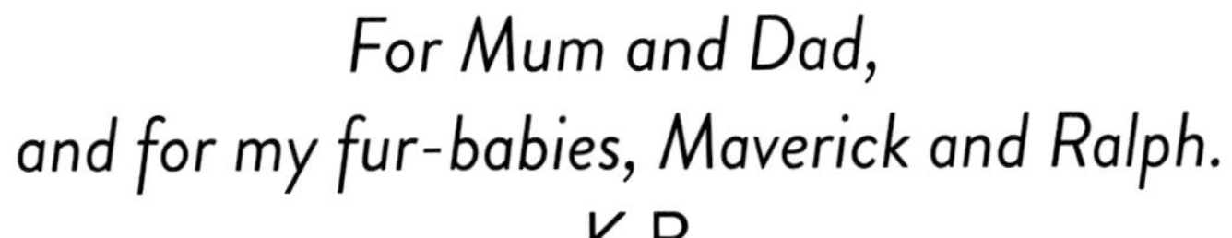

For Mum and Dad,
and for my fur-babies, Maverick and Ralph.
—K.B.

To my sister, Andrea, my best friend in the world.
She says she likes hearts and this book is full of them. Thanks for the laughs.
—M.O.

Pizza

LOVE is shown in many ways.
When we look closely, we
see it every day . . .

Gentle wake-up love.

Handmade lunch love.

"You're the best!" love.

Teach you to tie your shoelaces love.

"Want to wear my cape?" love.

A seat saved just
for you love.

“Cool outfit!” love.

"Let's do it together!" love.

“What a great effort!” love.

Sweet reminder love.

"Uh-oh. Want half?" love.

Surprise zoo time love.

“Bear hugs are the best!”
love.

"Need some help?" love.

"Look how you've improved!" love.

“Want to play fetch?” love.

No words needed love.

"I'll *try* to eat my veggies . . ."
love.

"Guess what's for dessert!" love.

“We can dry the dishes!”
love.

“You’re such good helpers!” love.

Super bubbly bubble bath love.

Messages in steam love.

Story time love.
TALES

Sweet dreams love.

Love is shown in many ways.
When we look closely,
we see it every day.

HOW DO **YOU** LOVE?

There is no *one* right way to show love. Everyone in your family, and everyone else you know, may express themselves differently in this regard.

As you've seen, we can let love out in many ways. How do you like to let the people or pets in your life know that you care about them? You might do some or all of the following:

SAY NICE THINGS.

You can help people and animals (and even plants!) feel good by using positive words and phrases in your interactions with them.

Give compliments or thanks, or tell others how you appreciate them.

Notice what people are good at and let them know what you admire most, such as your friend's clever craft skills, your sister's excellent hairstyle creations, or your uncle's booming laugh.

There are many ways to encourage and care through words.

GIVE A THOUGHTFUL GIFT.

You might like to indicate your love for someone by giving them a present.

Giving a gift you think they'll like shows that you've been thinking of them and that you're sharing the item as an expression of how you feel.

The presents you give out don't have to be expensive or cost anything at all. You can buy them, make them, or find them. Your gifts can come in all sorts of shapes and sizes, too.

It's all about providing that person in your life with a visual symbol of your feelings. Think about things they might like.

SPEND SPECIAL TIME TOGETHER.

You can show love by giving someone your undivided attention.

Spend time together talking and getting to know each other better. Really listen to what someone says. Try to notice how the other person is feeling.

Focus on who you're with, rather than on any other distracting things nearby. Enjoy being together, whether you're sitting quietly, playing a game, or taking a walk, for instance. You can do any activity that either or both of you like, but the point is to have fun with it together.

You and someone you love might also like to share things that happened in your days and talk about how you each feel about them.

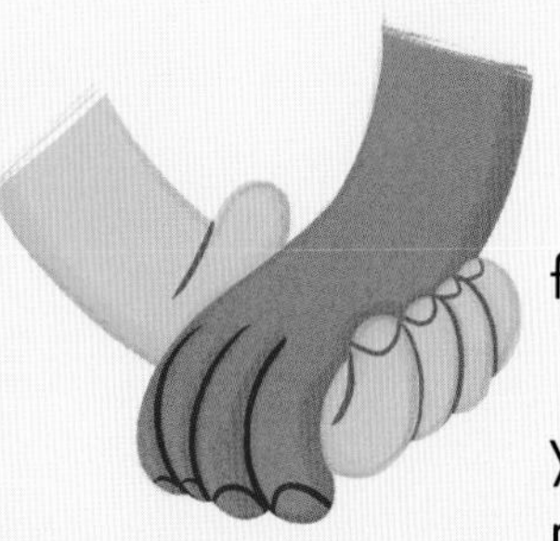

PROVIDE A KIND TOUCH.

Do you like to show you care by hugging people? Do you high-five your friends when things go well, or rub them on the back when they're sad?

Perhaps you let your little sister or brother sit on your lap for snuggles, or you stroke your cat each night before bed. You might hold hands with your parent or guardian when you're out or kiss them on the cheek when they drop you off for a play date.

Physical touch—provided it's okay with the other person or animal, of course—is another helpful way to communicate love.

DO SOMETHING NICE.

You might like to let someone know you love them by doing something nice for them—especially if it's something they don't like doing, are sick of doing, or find it hard to complete for themselves.

You could pack up your toys because you know your parents appreciate that, or pick vegetables from your grandparents' garden since it's hard for them to bend now with their sore knees.

Does your dog love tug-of-war? A game after school each day is a great way to show them you care.

These are just some of the ways
you can express your positive feelings.

Think about all the different ways
you already show your love.
Then, why not come up with new ideas
to try out in the future?